Once Upon a Buzzbee

GROSSET & DUNLAP
Penguin Young Readers Group
An Imprint of Penguin Random House LLC

ISBN 978-0-448-48744-1   10 9 8 7 6 5 4 3 2 1

It was nighttime at the hive. Pappa Bee was telling Buzzbee and Rubee a story about Pirate Bumble.

"Who's there?" Pappa Bee growled in his best pirate voice. "Who dares to knock on my door?"

Rubee and Buzzbee waited, shivering with excitement.

"*Rat-a-tat-tat!*" Pappa shouted.

Rat-a-tat-tat!

"I bet it's the pirate's shipmates!" Buzzbee said.

"Or maybe," said Pappa, "it's Captain Beakybee, the wickedest pirate that ever sailed the high seas!"

Rubee and Buzzbee's eyes grew wide as they waited to hear who was at Pirate Bumble's door.

"Or it could be the long-lost princess!" cried Rubee.

"And," said Pappa Bee, "we'll find out who it is tomorrow, in the next chapter of *Piraticus Tat-tat-icus*."

"Awwww, no!" Rubee and Buzzbee cried with disappointment.

At breakfast the next morning, Rubee and Buzzbee talked about Pappa's story.

"I can't wait to hear the end!" said Buzzbee.

"Mamma," said Rubee, "do you know who was knocking on Pirate Bumble's door?"

"I don't know," said Mamma. "We'll just have to wait for Pappa to tell us when he comes home later."

"Ohhh," Buzzbee groaned.

"Maybe the day will go faster if you're busy,"
Mamma suggested. "Why don't you two go
pick up my egg order at Ant Hill Stores?"

On the way to the store, Rubee and Buzzbee tried to guess the ending of the story.

"I think it was the long-lost princess," said Rubee.

"Princesses don't go '*rat-a-tat-tat*' on doors," Buzzbee replied.

"Hello, Rubee. Hello, Buzzbee," said Katypillar. She was busy with her own shopping. "Did I hear you talking about a princess?"

"It's a story Pappa was telling us," said Rubee.

"I like stories!"
Vince Ant cried.

"Me too," said Millice Ant.
"Oh, please tell us the story!"

Buzzbee told them the whole story of Pirate Bumble, right up to the part where there was a knock at the door.

Rat-a-tat-tat!

"It could be his pirate shipmates," said Buzzbee.

"Or the long-lost princess," said Rubee. "We have to wait until Pappa comes home tonight to hear the rest."

"I hope it's the princess," said Katypillar.

On the way home, Buzzbee and Rubee were still buzzing about Pappa's story.

"I'm a princess. I'm a princess. *Rat-a-tat-tat!* A long-lost princess!" sang Rubee.

"Princesses don't even go '*rat-a-tat-tat*,'" Buzzbee complained. "Pirates do!"

They buzzed straight past Postman Spider. "What's this about pirates?" Postman Spider asked them.

Buzzbee and Rubee told him Pappa's story about Pirate Bumble.

Postman Spider looked serious. "So, it might be wicked Captain Beakybee! Who is it? Who's at the door?"

"We don't know!" said Buzzbee.

Postman Spider sighed. "When does your Pappa get home?"

Later that day, Buzzbee and Rubee waited eagerly for Pappa to come home.

"Mamma," called Buzzbee, "when will Pappa get home?"

"Soon," Mamma replied.

Buzzbee sighed. "How soon?"

A moment later, Katypillar arrived. Then Postman Spider, too!

Everyone wanted Pappa to come home and finish his story.

When Pappa finally walked in, everyone shouted and cheered.

"Are we having a party?" Pappa asked.

"Everyone wants to hear about Pirate Bumble, Pappa! We need to know who's going '*rat-a-tat-tat*' on his door!"

"So? Who was it? Who was at the door?" asked Vince and Millice.

"Is it the princess?" asked Katypillar.

"I can't wait to hear!" said Postman Spider.

"Uh . . . ummm . . . I don't know . . . ," said Pappa. "I . . . uh . . . I sort of made the story up."

Everyone gasped. "What?"

"You made it up?" cried Buzzbee.

"All stories are made up," said Pappa. "That's half the fun! They can end however we like."

"Pirate Bumble began to roar.
'Who's there?! Who dares to knock on my door?'"

The room was silent.
Everyone's eyes
were fixed on Pappa.

He continued his tale. "'We do! We do!' lots of voices replied. 'Happy birthday, Bumble!'" Pappa sang out. "It was all Pirate Bumble's shipmates. They had come to wish him a happy birthday!"

"But what about the princess?" asked Katypillar.

"I know!" said Buzzbee, finishing Pappa's exciting tale. "They all sailed off on a new adventure and found the long-lost princess on a desert island!"

"And the princess was so happy to see them," Mamma said, handing out treats, "she baked everyone their very favorite treasure-trove cupcakes."

"It was Pirate Bumble's best birthday ever!" Buzzbee added.

"The end," said Pappa.